ANGRY ARTHUR

for
Tremayne
and
Piers

A Red Fox Book

Published by Random House Children's Books
61-63 Uxbridge Road, London W5 5SA

A division of Random House UK Ltd
London Melbourne Sydney Auckland
Johannesburg and agencies throughout the world

First published in 1982 by Andersen Press Ltd

Red Fox edition 1993

12 14 16 18 20 19 17 15 13

Printed in Hong Kong

RANDOM HOUSE UK Limited Reg. No. 954009

ISBN 0 09 919661 1

www.kidsatrandomhouse.co.uk

ANGRY ARTHUR

Text by Hiawyn Oram
Pictures by Satoshi Kitamura

RED FOX

Once there was a boy called Arthur.
He wanted to stay up and watch
the western on T.V.

"No," said his mother,
"it's too late. Go to bed."
"I'll get angry," said Arthur.
"Get angry,"
said his mother.

So he did. Very, very angry.
He got so angry that his anger became a stormcloud
exploding thunder and lightning and hailstones.

"That's enough,"
said his mother.
But it wasn't.

Arthur's anger became a hurricane hurling rooftops and chimneys and church spires.

"That's enough,"
said his father.
But it wasn't.

Arthur's anger became a typhoon
tipping whole towns
into the seas.

"That's enough," said his grandfather.
But it wasn't.

Arthur's anger became an earth tremor cracking the surface of the earth like a giant cracking eggs.
"That's enough," said his grandmother.
But it wasn't.

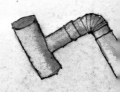

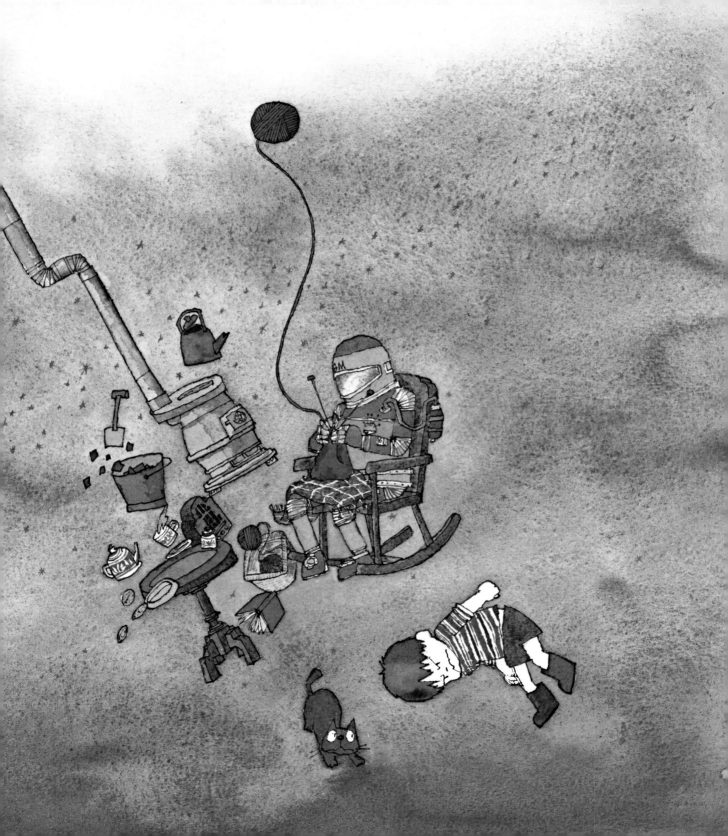

Arthur's anger became a universequake

and the earth and the moon

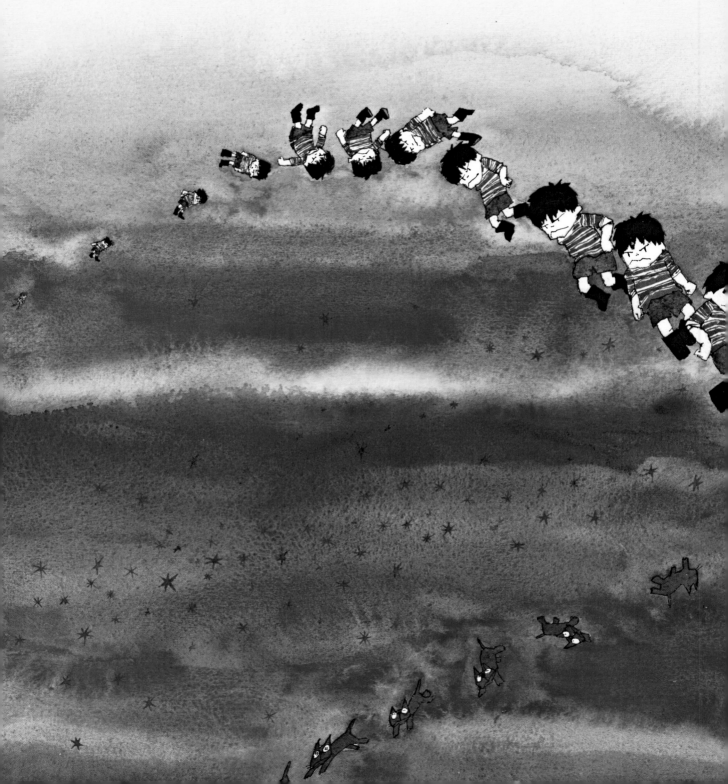

and the stars and the planets,

Arthur's country and Arthur's town, his street, his house, his garden and his bedroom

were nothing more
than bits in space.

Arthur sat on a piece of Mars and thought.
He thought and thought.

"Why was I so angry?" he thought.
He never did remember.
Can you?

More Red Fox picture books
for you to enjoy

ELMER
by David McKee 0099697203

MUMMY LAID AN EGG
by Babette Cole 0099299119

RUNAWAY TRAIN
by Benedict Blathwayt 0099385716

DOGGER
by Shirley Hughes 009992790X

WHERE THE WILD THINGS ARE
by Maurice Sendak 0099408392

OLD BEAR
by Jane Hissey 0099265761

MISTER MAGNOLIA
by Quentin Blake 0099400421

ALFIE GETS IN FIRST
by Shirley Hughes 0099855607

OI! GET OFF OUR TRAIN
by John Burningham 009985340X

GORGEOUS
by Caroline Castle and Sam Childs 0099400766